The Adventures of Magellan

T.L. Mann

Illustrated by Victor Guiza

Outskirts Press, Inc.
Denver, Colorado

This is a work of fiction. The events and characters described herein are imaginary and are not intended to refer to specific places or living persons. The opinions expressed in this manuscript are solely the opinions of the author and do not represent the opinions or thoughts of the publisher. The author has represented and warranted full ownership and/or legal right to publish all the materials in this book.

Outskirts Press, Inc.
http://www.outskirtspress.com

ISBN: 978-1-4327-3490-9

PRINTED IN THE UNITED STATES OF AMERICA

This Book Belongs to:

____

Hi, my name is Magellan, and I'm going to take you on some wonderful adventures, but first, I need to tell you how it all began....

Magellan
United States
of America

My life started out on a beautiful 150 acre farm owned by the McKenzies. My mom took great care of me and my five brothers and sisters, but I was the one she worried about the most. You see, I loved to explore, and with 150 acres surrounding me, there was a lot to see and do. Every day I attempted to break away from my family for a few hours and explore my surroundings, always hoping to see new things, and this particular day was no different.

I had been born and lived at the farm for eight weeks now, and the McKenzies were looking for new homes for me and my brothers and sisters. Although I was a little sad to leave my family, I was excited about the new adventure. Sometime around noon, a nice couple came to the farm to choose a puppy to take home. Stephanie and Michael Patterson were undecided as to which one of the puppies they wanted to adopt. Although they liked all of my brothers and sisters, Stephanie could not decide which one to choose.

As Mrs. Patterson bent down to play with the puppies, I was coming back from my daily adventure. I had been watching a fish swim in the pond, and when I tried to put my paw in to play, I fell in the pond.

I knew my mom would not be pleased with what had happened, and when I approached, I could see the disappointment on her face. I also noticed that we had visitors, so I went running to greet them. I heard Mrs. McKenzie apologize for my appearance, as she explained to the Pattersons about my tendency to wander off. After I had spent several minutes with the Pattersons, they decided to take me home. Mrs. Patterson said that I was just what they were looking for as an addition to their family.

I said goodbye to my brothers and sisters, and jumped in the car. During the entire trip, I looked out the window. There was so much to see outside the farm: tall buildings, people jogging, children playing, even dogs just like me being taken for walks. I couldn't wait to see my new home, and when we pulled up, I was surprised. Although the yard wasn't as big as the McKenzies' farm, I knew it would take me weeks to explore everything both inside and outside the house. As the Pattersons took me inside, they were discussing what to name me. They had said a few names: Lucky, Champ, Baxter, none of which I liked. Then, Stephanie said she thought I should be named Magellan, since I liked to explore. As soon as she said it, I knew the name fit, and I started barking to express my satisfaction.

Several weeks went by, and I grew to love my new family. They made sure I had enough to eat and gave me great toys to play with and a nice cozy bed in which to sleep. They even had a special name tag made for my collar, shaped like a globe.

During the week, they both left the house to go to work, which was when my explorations took place. One evening, while the Pattersons were eating dinner, and I was resting in the kitchen, after a busy day, I heard Mr. Patterson say that we would be moving. His job was requiring him to move to another country, and we would be moving in a few weeks to a place called China. I couldn't believe that I was going to get the chance, once again, to explore new territory.

Several weeks passed, and then we were on our way to the airport, to travel to our new home. Not only was I getting to ride in the car again, but I was going to get to fly on a plane. I was placed in a compartment underneath the plane, in my crate, before taking off, since animals are not permitted to fly inside the plane. While in the cargo hold, I met another dog, named Salvatore, who was flying home to Italy. I started to get a little concerned, because if the plane was going to Italy, how was I getting to China?

When the plane landed, my fears were confirmed. I had landed in Italy, and the Pattersons were nowhere to be found. My crate must have been loaded on the wrong plane. Salvatore invited me to ride along with his owner and visit this country he called Italy. The door to my crate had opened during the landing, so this gave me the perfect opportunity to escape. I knew I would eventually meet up with my family, so I decided to accept his invitation, and hid inside a piece of his owner's luggage. My new adventure was about to begin…

INFORMATION
ARRIVALS
ARRIVI
ARRIVEES
LLEGADAS
FORZA AZZURI

LaVergne, TN USA
04 November 2009
162942LV00002B